Rush

Of

Many

Waters

Also by Pauly Hart

Rush of Many Waters:
Volume Seven
By Pauly Hart

Contents

Shorts

Shamsiel's large shoulders were not tired, but they would have been, if he had been a human. The bright blue angel had nothing else to do but to watch and think. There was no exertion, no weariness when it came to the beings in his realm. They did not grow fat or slothful in their position. Yet, in spite of the natural patience of his kind, Shamsiel had indeed grown tired. Tired of watching his friends walk to and fro about the earth. Tired and a little jealous perhaps of their freedom, a freedom that he once had himself. He longed to return to his old position... To regain what he had lost.

Azazel had come to him again, as he did quite often. Azazel was in a position where he could walk the earth whenever he pleased. Azazel was a Watcher of Mankind. Not merely a watcher of the second men, but all of the people upon the earth... Those created from the Word, and those created from the Breath. Azazel had many questions for Shamsiel, about the wanderings to and fro of people of the earth, and their dealings with Adam and his family. Many of the other Watchers came and went, always asking, asking, asking, and he always answered.

There were two of them who stood there. He and Metatron, but Metatron never said a word to the visitors, for he reported directly to the Book, and when the visitors left to go wander again, Shamsiel was left alone with his stoic companion, whose face was always set to the east.

Azazel, with his purple glimmering wings, Kokabiel, in his gold cloak, and Semjaza, of the purest white and yellow - would flutter in off of the wind. They would question Shamsiel night and day until he had told all that he knew of all that he saw. What man had been doing, who married who, when the rains would come... Shamsiel did nothing to hold back any truth, for truth was all that he knew. He had been created this way, as had all of them... To always speak what you know.

"Tell us Shamsiel." Azazel would ask again and again. "What do you see here? What do you know of these days, of these things?" So many questions, so often, so urgently. Azazel was like an empty vessel, always needing to be filled.

What was seen, what had happened... All would know of it eventually. All would tell of it, so what was the matter if Shamsiel told of it first? This was the mind of an obedient guard.

And so, in a full force of evil, when that 'Dark Day' came, where the son took up a stone to kill his brother... After that, Azazel brought Semjaza and Kokabiel, and he was forced to tell, again and again, every part of the story. No detail was amiss. Azazel was almost drunk on hearing the tale. He made Shamsiel tell it once more... His eyes, full of lust, of wanton need, watching Shamsiel's eyes and lips when he talked. To know fully. To know every last detail. He wanted it all. He needed it all.

Two

Shamsiel reminisced. He remembered the times gone by, when he and Hasdiel were chief aids to Uriel. Uriel was one of the twelve guards that served as the voice. Uriel was among the four who held the winds of the earth, who had held the season of summer. Uriel also served as the Apocalypse presiding over Samael, the chief Angel of Death. He held the key to the Pit and was responsible for the entrance to Hades on the last day of days. Shamsiel and Hasdiel had looked up to him, serving in Uriel's shadow. Shamsiel shone like a jewel in the light of Uriel, and when Shamsiel was chosen to be one of the angels who stood guard at this place, he had thanked Uriel for the assignment. Hasdiel had been handed the lonely post of tending Saturn, while Shamsiel had his sentinel duty next to Metatron. He did not know what he had done to deserve this or if it was any better than being in one of the upper heavens, guarding one of the wandering stars.

When the others came to ask questions, as always, Metatron did not give his opinion. Not of the job, nor of anything else. Metatron was Metatron alone. An enigma in a puzzle in a riddle. Enormous to be sure, the second largest angel in heaven. He was the definition of imposition. People from a distance, if they could see him, always knew that the guards were there. Metatron, glowing with the red fire of the sun, was almost as bright as the face of HIM.

Once, on a day like any other, Metatron and Shamsiel were watching Adam and his sons work in the field with their wives. Shamsiel had noticed that Adam's grief grew with every day that passed. Adam had not come up today to remember. Adam used to come by Shamsiel daily and stare with longing past him, and remember what he had lost. And though Adam could not actually see inside, for it had been hidden from man, he would steal glances back and think of their last day there. The day when HE had cut open a Capri and laid it out on the ground. The blood covenant that HE cut with Adam had served as both the sacrifice for sin as well as to clothe the man Adam and his wife Issah.

The people of the earth had come to trade, down by their newly built houses. The earth people had brought with them their very few precious belongings. Almost dumb with awe at the sight of Adam, they groveled with their nuts and berries and wild eggs. Adam and his wife would trade grains and milk from their work with the land. Adam was in charge of the farms and the flocks, and also of building the enclosures they had come to dwell in, while she was in charge of maintaining everything inside of the dwellings. Shamsiel saw that the houses they built reflected the houses in the hosts of heaven, and envied Adam and his genius for their building. They were poor reflections, but they had achieved this knowledge from nowhere, simply the residual breath of HIM.

Eve had gained her new name when they had their children... Able and Cain. It was a hideous process to be born the way earth people were born, but this was the process that HE had ordained for them now that they were outside.

Adam had taken her name away when this happened. Issah meant "It is another one like me," Eve meant "Here is the mother of my children." She had changed since she had been forced out. She never came near, but once, while she was walking by, she stopped and peered right into Shamsiel's eyes and wept bitter tears.

Three

Shamsiel watched the world grow and flourish around him, one microsecond out of phase with the rest of creation. There, around him sprung the settlement, village, town and eventually the fortified metropolis of Eridu, the first town of the second men. The sons and daughters of the earth men and the second men had bred. Adam's third son, Seth had married one of the more beautiful daughters of the chiefs of the towns around Eridu. "The sons and daughters born to them were almost like pure second men, but not quite. Adam's line continued to have children, an enormous amount of children even, and the new sons: Enos, Kenan, Mahal, and Jared were the rulers of them all. They spread out, and the entirety of the world became their vast empire.

And Shamsiel heard tales of other men. Not the first men, nor the second men of Seth, but of the cursed second men: The man they called Cain. Of tall structures, buildings, ziggurats, and great wonders... of tools, instruments, weapons, and even things that he wished he had not have heard, but he had.

Azazel came again. He had brought Semjaza with him, and for three days he told Shamsiel stories of life outside Eridu. Then they began to question him. Questions of allegiance, obedience, and temptation. Shamsiel questioned them as well. Of their dealings with the first and second men, of the buildings they are constructing, and of the gods they were creating. Semjaza said that they too were creating their own men. Not of the Adam, but of the Hadam, the people of the earth that were built by HIM on the sixth day.

They were built to have dominion over the earth, and Semjaza said that the Angels were built to have dominion over them. So then, if the Watchers were built to have dominion over the men, then how can they do that in their given role? We should shake off the role and strive to become more like HIM. Wasn't that the point of HIS creation? To grow, learn, adapt, and to evolve? Semjaza and Azazel wore him down with their false friendship and lengthy discourse. Though it seemed it would be sensible to disagree with them, Shamsiel's heart was faint within him, and he found himself agreeing with them on some small matters, and even larger matters as they persisted. Such things sounded true, yet the fiery face of Metatron said otherwise.

Metatron looked at him. His eyes betrayed his mouth. He was in contact with HIM and he told HIM everything. Everything Shamsiel had done there, Metatron knew, and when he knew, then HE knew, for there were no secrets in HIS presence.

Four

In the midst of the discourse, in mid-sentence, a boom from the sky made them all shudder and turn. There, a black and red flame cloud tore across the heavens like a comet, but a thousand times faster. A long tail was arching across the sky, blackening all the blue around it, and the wake of the falling object was black soot and death. Faster and closer it ripped through the sky, visible only to the creatures who lived in the spirit. With a forceful slam on the ground, directly in front of them, the black figure landed. Like a cloud into the ground around him, the ash fell off him and landed in a soft rain covering everything around. Suddenly Azazel pulled out his whip with a cracking sound and Semjaza drew his immense swords, thinking that this was something else. An ambush. But the dark creature did not turn to face them. His enormous black wings, beat once, shuttered and then folded. With one finger, he pulled up the mask he used for carrying out his tasks and exposed his face. He wasn't here to kill, but to deliver a message.

Samael the Destroyer, The Angel of Death stood before Shamsiel, his black eyes like the cosmos. Diamond sword in the left hand, and trumpet in the right. He lifted the trumpet and blew three times into the sky. The earth shook with the resonation and birds fled the trees. Although the men of the city below us had not heard it with their ears, their hearts melted like wax inside of their chests. Whatever anyone was doing in the world, they stopped. Somehow all things knew that a profound change was occurring. Not understanding what any of it could mean, they continued on, bent in their daily tasks. The world went on for them.

But not for Shamsiel. For the destroying angel, Samael, had come to banish him. Shamsiel had chosen, in one brief second, to question and doubt HIM, and for that, there was no forgiveness. With an unearthly scream, Shamsiel's wings caught fire, twisted themselves and fell off, one by one, shriveling and drying up as they went. The bluish-green feathers that once adorned them, now turned brown and faded into the dust. His blue tone took on a darker hue and his brilliant sword now seemed to suck up the light around it, instead of giving off its own. His eyes, surprised and shamed, looked deep into Samael's. Shamsiel had been banished forever. The Death Angel said nothing, merely holstered his trumpet, and pointed his long arm away, towards the city, and away from the gates of the Garden of Eden.

"Or so the story goes," Azrael said, as he stirred the embers of the dying fire in front of him.

"What happened to Shamsiel, daddy?" the little boy asked. He had been lying in his lap, playing with a bird his father had made him.

"I met your mother," Azrael, as he was now called, said smiling. He scooped up the boy and they headed home. The bird flew from his hands, off into the night.

It was a two cigarette problem. He knew that. His mind told him that. The only problem was that there were no cigarettes. There hadn't been cigarettes for three years now. That didn't take away from the fact that it was still a two cigarette problem.

"Gold." he sighed, and leaned back on his stool, staring at the ceiling. "Gold, gold, ev'ywhere and notta drop ta drink."

"You would think that they would just suck the planet dry and be done with it." the man behind the bar said, picking up the leftover drinks on the table.

"Leave 'em." the man said. "I still got some ice left."

"Suit yerself Jaf." the man behind the bar said. "You wanna refill?"

"Nah." said the man on the stool. "I'm good."

Pool balls sounded behind them with a wooden *chok*. You could hear the ball rolling down the chute and then into the return slot.

"That's my game Smitty." said the man who had just sunk the eight ball. "You owe me ten."

"Bull-honkey!" the other man said, slamming his pool cue down. "It was five!"

Jaf leaned back, putting all legs of his stool on the ground and slowly stood. Everyone suddenly became quiet.

The man behind the bar paid him no attention as Jaf placed his hat on his head and slowly made towards the door. All eyes were on him. He was the man in charge.

"Be outside fer a bit. Prolly gonna be a minnit." he said, and stepped onto the porch.

The view was what you would expect. A golden sunset over the vast desert. The saloon was the last building in town before the great expanse. Markova was a big place, and Jaf hated every square inch of it. This was probably why he had decided to blow the whole place up, once he got his crew back on the space-boat. If he got rid of the entire planet, the gold would be gone too, and then whatever they'd taken would be worth a whole heck of a lot more. He needed a cigarette though. Two of them.

The small cloud on the horizon that he hadn't cared about moments ago was not getting any smaller. It could be riders from Markova. He went back inside. He hated cops.

"Cookie!" He called to the man behind the bar, "You expectin' company?" He asked as he held open the door.

The man behind the bar furrowed his brow and slowly shook his head.

"Nope." He said. "Prolly could be some o' dem outlanders I seen up on Jewlit Ridge yesterday."

"Or it could be One Time." Smitty said from the pool table.

'One Time' referred to the Markova Marshalls. Smitty had a "hankerin for hatin on 'em somethin fierce." As he would say. He was from Old Earth and was a wanted man on four continents.

"Saddle up!" said the man at the door. "Get yer guns and make em on hot. I ain't takin no chances."

Five minutes later a Damram and five Self-Units came to a rest in front of the rusted out metal shed that bore the sign: "Cookie's Cookies: A Five Star Joint, Best Beer In The Outer Ring." It was a real shit-hole Commander Goraw noticed. Behind the building was a K49 Cruiser with a junket booster hanging off the side. Why would an atmosphere car need a scramjet? You never knew about the weird folk out here. But it was better here looking into things than with his old partner Yoq. She would just shoot everyone and ask questions later. He was glad that he had been moved out here in the boonies and left her on Old Earth.

"You three men around back. Bippy, you're with me. I'm not taking any chances." He motioned to the only other actual man that had come with him. The three 'men' were Syntho's. They would follow orders without question. The Damram stayed where it had parked. He spoke to it.

"Active command Goraw H-4. Hold ground." He barked.

"AFFIRMATIVE." The hulking machine said and unfolded itself into something like a huge turret with eight guns.

Commander Goraw waited until the three men were in position. So far the building had shown no signs of life.

"We gonna give 'em hell boss?" Bippy asked.

"Nah. I just want to get myself a beer," he said as he wandered in.

Inside, nothing was moving. The pale dust still hung in the air from when he and his gang had come strolling up, but the tables were all overturned, facing him. Even an old pool table was tipped towards him.

After a long pause Goraw decided to break the ice. He took a long roll of his mouth, working up some saliva and spit on the ground. "Sure would be a shame to break that beautiful pool table."

A muffled voice answered him. "We ain't lookin' for no trouble Sheriff! We aim to just drink our beer in peace and mosey on outta here."

Goraw smiled. "Then why you acting all suspicious? I'm not here to serve warrants or dispense justice. I just need to… How do you say it here? 'Wet my whistle.'" He slowly walked over to the vacant bar and leaned over. The man behind the bar was on the floor with his hands over his head.

"Excuse me? May I purchase a drink?" Goraw asked him.

Trembling, Cookie looked up and slowly stood. His dusty gray hair and pale blue eyes shimmered, he was shaking so badly.

"S-sure." He grabbed a glass, spat on it, wiped it off and poured a fresh brew. The glass fogged up as the cold drink roiled and settled within.

He slowly placed it down and said: "Fifteen-fifty if you please."

Goraw held out his wrist and the man behind the bar touched the reader to it. *Beep*. The man behind the bar took a step back and slowly went back down to the ground, hands again above his head.

Jaffy's legs were cramping. "That dangnab cop just sittin at the bar doin nothin but slurpin on the brewski." He thought. He called out to him.

"You got any idea who I is?" Jaf asked the cop.

"Nope," the cop said.

"Then why is ya here?" Jaf asked.

"Well. I was told to come find some thieves. Are you a thief?" He said.

Another pause.

"Mebbe I am... What was stolen?" Jaf said.

"Just some planet-gold. Nothing much. But enough to hide on board of a K49. Juuust enough - actually." Goraw smiled. He didn't think he would have to shoot anybody today. This was going well.

The bullet that hit him in the back was a smaller caliber and it would have gone through regular armor. But it was a good thing that he was not wearing regular armor today. The next bullets went into bottles of Rum, Scotch and Mirror, in that order.

Yet even before the second, third, and fourth bullets had hit, Goraw was on the move. With a leap, he pushed off from the ground, knocking the stool over behind him. Half a flip to the ceiling and another half to the ground, he landed behind the back of the pool table.

A startled man, gun in hand blinked at him in surprise and seconds later was even more startled as Goraw's stick-net threw him to the ground in a muffled *whump*.

Leaping again up and over to the front of the pool table, Goraw came down in a crouch, low enough to be out of sight.

"Boss is taking fire!" came from outside. "Prepare to engage the assaila-!"

"Stand down! Stand down!" Goraw shouted as loud as he could, although he didn't need to. The heads up system allowed them all to talk to each other in whispers. "I want this one for myself!" he said and smiled to himself.

Bullets sailed over the pool table, and some into it. He was tracking the shots. Nothing big was being used. All small caliber, but they all had metal piercing jackets. At least these knuckle-heads didn't use incendiary rounds. He very much disliked being on fire. He jumped up in a spinning backflip. He had judged correctly where to land and was able to envelop another man with the netting. *Thwap* went the man as he fell to the ground. According to sensors, there were two men left, excluding the man behind the bar. Maybe they would listen to reason now.

"Two of your men are down thief! Do you want to talk about this or what?" He asked.

A moment of silence. Too long of a moment. He thought if he could just get to-

The electric jolt that threw Goraw over was horrific. His helmet slammed shut and he wet himself inside his self-unit, cursed and rebooted. When a self-unit is shut down for whatever reason, the helmet always slams shut. He might as well be inside of a tank at this point, he was so well protected. The man who had hit him was quickly fashioning some sort of restraint. The second man jumped up to help him while he lay there helpless. His suit would reboot and pretty soon he would mop the floor with these guys.

"Boss?" Bippy called from outside. "You want some help now or what?"

Reboot complete. "No. This is mine. You boys stay put. I almost have them."

But he couldn't move. The Lectrowire restraint was bound around his ankles and his wrists and then joined together. It was causing his suit to brown out. It kept pulsing small charges through his suit. His systems were on, but didn't have enough power to give him control over anything.

The two men drug him behind the pool table and looked at him.

"Reckon I stole that gold, do ya?" Jaf asked.

"Yes. And you are under arrest." Goraw said through clenched teeth. The tiny loudspeaker on the outside of his helmet transmitted his consternation.

Jaf pointed to the other two. "Get 'em outta those traps." He told Smitty, "but bring me my case first."

Smitty scrambled away and was back moments later with a silver case.

"Imma go get em unstuck boss."

"Make it quick."

Jaf opened it up and pressed in a sequence of numbers and hit a red button.

"I ain't dyin here copper." He said very slowly. "I aim to blow up this whole stinking asteroid."

"It's officially a planet now." Goraw said. "And how are you going to blow it up? You can't even win in a decent bar fight."

Jaf laughed. "I got you didn't I?" and spat again.

Just then Smitty came scrambling back with a knife. "Boss, they's five more outside. One of them's a big old stinkin robot!" Smitty had a wild look in his eye. He had never liked robots.

"No matter," said Jaf, pointing with the gun, "Go free them other two and get back here." A pause. "So… By the way…" He tapped Goraw on the helmet with his gun. "You got any cigarettes?"

Goraw said nothing. And Jaf didn't pursue the question any further. They both waited while Smitty performed his task, then Goraw spoke. "Listen. You're surrounded. You're stupid. And you can't blow up a planet. That's the craziest and dumbest thing I've ever heard of." Goraw said.

Jaf eyed Goraw in a slow squint, as if trying to read his mind, glancing over now and again watching his comrades being freed. "Get to the windows! I'm gonna get us outta here one way or t'other!"

When they were up, Jaf leaned in. "You think I'm just some hick? Some hayseed out here doin a bit o' rough-neckin and then off to another shit hole? No sir. I'm a Second Level Pyrotechnic Volcanologist. Studied on Old Earth too. I've been here mining now for the last eight years. Markova boys want to pull me out and send me packing. But not before I give em a little sumtin sumtin." Jaf smiled and looked over at the case.

"We got three minutes and thirty two seconds left. Thirty one. Thirty." Then: "Pull your boys away, or we all get the big number right up the ass. This ain't suicide mister law-man, I just need a really big bargaining chip."

Goraw was speechless. Who in their right mind would blow up an entire planet? There were women and children here. It was the most insane thing he had ever heard in his entire life. There was no way he had a button that would blow up the world. What tomfoolery. There was no way. Was there? He had been here a long time, and he must have been down to the core... Maybe... He swallowed before he spoke.

"Goraw Delta. Goraw Delta. Cut the cake." he said. But he didn't say it on the speaker. He said it to Bippy. There was a loud *click*, a *chunt* and a *whir* from outside. The hail of bullets that ripped into the building was something out of a dream. Like a chainsaw through willing wood, the building cut in half. Shutters of metal and shrapnel rang out everywhere as the bullets continued. Glass and wood became almost liquid and dust. The sheer power of the barrage was deafening. When the roof and the entire top half of the building caved in around them, it crushed everything.

He was in darkness then. The lectrowire shorted out and he was free again. He stood with a great effort, moving the roofing around him. A trembling hand, Jaf's hand, rose shaking, raising itself out of the dust and grabbed his leg. Goraw slid the roof off and let it land on the pile. The hand spasmed and lay still.

His guess was that there was around one minute left to try to defuse the bomb.

Where was it! Where was it! SHIT! Whe-

Ah.

There it was. He picked it up as he stood.

But he was wrong.

There were only three seconds left on the clock.

There wasn't even any time to-

Loren

All he remembered was the fire. The sky. Rain had come in the form of burning brands of death. The fire had come and taken him away. It seemed like so long ago. Where was he? Looking around at his surroundings, it seemed so peaceful, so tranquil. A clean river. No fire. This was a good sign. He tried to arise. Shaking, he fell back down, his teeth grinding on the rocks. Slowly then, first his arms then legs. then to stand. And sway. Quickly, he found a rock to lean on. He looked at himself. Adorned in blackened armor, a large scabbard hanging from his left hip, now attached intricately to his guard belt hung Gildarim, his only friend at the moment.

As he reached for the sword, the man calling himself Loren glances into the still pool and sees a shabby figure, tall and burnt. He grabs the sword. Once flaxen-yellow hair has been charred dark by the forces behind his former imprisonment. The burned armor that was once golden hangs all about his lanky figure. Breastplate, gauntlets, shoulder-pieces, neck-bracer, guard belt, bracers, leggings, and boots. Various pockets and folds are in the clothes beneath the armor. He has no idea what he is carrying, has he need for anything else?

He gazes at his face. At first he appears handsome, but he gazes closer. Haggard and skinny, his face is laced with almost invisible scars. Crisscrossing his terrible face, his eyes are black. Terribly black. But wait? A yellow glow. Now gold. Now glowing. He pulls away. *"Hmmm."* He thinks. *"Not what I thought."*

The chill of the water came seemingly into his very soul, awakening the vision he had from his birth. A Ring. A Tower. A Quake. The Fall. His heart. Standing, he looked around. Not seeing his horse. *"Do I have a horse?"* he wondered to himself. He began to climb up the embankment. Something cold was on his neck. A thick gold torc-like necklace adorned him. It was of dragonish design. Even the connection was of the Dragon's head biting his tail. "Hmmm..." he said aloud. "I don't remember that at all." Loren grumbles something unintelligible and tucks the torc once again into his bracer. He does not know where it came from or how he owns it, and suspicions are terrible things. Now where was that horse of his?

Loren thought for a moment. "Hello? Anyone?" he yelled... Nothing. Taking the last remains of his strength, he walked upstream towards the silence.

The man naming himself Loren stands with his head cocked to one side as if listening. He looked at himself. His armor and hair blackened. By whom? This fascinates him. Fingering the hilt of his sword, he studies the air, as if it would speak to him. "No fire… Hmmm, good, good, good." He mumbles. Then: "I must go."

He shambles towards the woods. Eyeing the mystery within, he wonders if this could be the reason for him finding himself here. Well, an adventure would do him some good. Perhaps it would help him remember something.

Something? Anything! When was the last time he had looked at a blue sky? Where was his horse? When had he company last? When was it that he looked on the face of another and did not see the hateful tower that had imprisoned him those many decades?

Prison? Indeed, had he been imprisoned? Hmmm. No matter now. Freedom took its gracious wings and caressed his face like a newborn. Freedom tasted good. Drawing his sword he thrust it heavenward. The golden hilt turned black, as if alive, and the blackness covered the blade down to the tip until...

"Abla Kine' Tsedkenu Elelyon Gnoscos," he let tear from his ragged burnt-away throat. Suddenly, as if transported far away, he stood on a green-gold tower. Bricks and mortar had fallen away, and all that was left was the small platform he stood upon. Shaky and unsafe. Fire rained down from the sky. Inky darkness licked the Earth well below him. Shapes that have no name moved within. There was no wind. No sound. Only the eerie whistle of the brands of fire making their mark on the undeserving ground. And then, in a rush of wind and sound he was returned to the present. The sounds of the river pushed him to the ground and things were back where they had been. It was if he had never left. Perhaps he hadn't left, perhaps he had.

The man naming himself Loren was steaming, as if he had been immersed in magma.

He walked for what seemed days up the stream. Camping by the river on the third night, he riffled through his belongings. He had not eaten or slept or seen his horse, for that matter.

A map, a compass, a medicine bag containing several herbs and elixirs, several coins made of gold and platinum, and a dagger that glowed orange when he touched it. But no food.

His thoughts were unreadable. His mind fixed. "Follow the river." he said to the himself, "It has to lead somewhere."

He thought of his vision. It had seemed that he had seen much, much more than just the vision. Perhaps it was that others had seen him. Yes, that was it. Others had known of his vision, but had not been aware of who he was. *That* was very strange. He wondered if they knew his thoughts too.

Suddenly before him were voices. Four or five. No, six voices. Coming closer. Jumping away from the small trail that lead along the side of the river, he grabbed himself close to a tree. "Don't see me. I am not ready." He mumbled. Closing his eyes, he could still "see" them as they walked by, unaware. Then minutes later, silence.

Air! Fire! He fell away from the tree as if in anguish. The whole world was on fire. Reaching the river, he plunged his hand into it to drink, only to find that his hand upon contact with the water, set the whole area steaming! He must be on fire. No. He checked. Not on fire, but incredibly hot. He sat for quite some time until he could move again. There must be some way to make the fires subside.

Hmmm. He had heard six voices yet there were more footprints than that.

No matter. Following someone would be an interesting departure from following the stream and may serve as a salve to the torment of his mind. He would follow them for a while. They might prove interesting. Being around people now seemed... Right.

After a while the foot-path had grown into a larger lane and signs of civilization were more apparent. "*Where would these take me, if I followed them?*" he wondered.

And follow them he did.

They came to a funeral plot, and there was a service underway. As he looked at them from the distance he could make out none of their faces, for every time he gazed at someone, a thick black veil would be pulled down over them as if in a dream. There was something wrong with him. Was it the fires again? Why did he have to suffer even now? Had not he suffered enough in his imprisonment? And where was his horse?

Wait! His horse was there with the people! They had stolen it from him and were using it to haul the casket that they were now lowering into the ground. The people around the horse seemed like they loved the body that they were burying. They loved him. Him. And it all came back.

There was no possible way, but he felt as if he knew the grievers. He made bold and walked towards them, his footsteps almost scorching the earth below him. Thirty feet and they had not seen him. Twenty. Ten. He was now beside them and they did not know he was there. How could they not? His horse, head hung low, did not even greet him, and he had raised it since it was a foal. But wait. The crest on the casket looked familiar. It was his own!

The people at the funeral were his family. They loved him. They loved Loren. They loved Loren? Yes. His squire and his company as well as his sister, Ardu. They had taken his body from the battlefield and now had brought him to his hometown in Kalimsa. He was witnessing his own funeral.

He had been imprisoned, true. But it had been in hellfire. He had returned as a devil, to accomplish all that he could not have done when he had mortal flesh. Turning from his earthen self and strode off to find out what that was.

Poems

flair for her
flair for her
why do i even care for her
blonde hair dove
brown eyes love
why do i even dare for her
wish i could
thought i should
why, why, why

question one
question two
why do i care for her
lives that touch
futures changed
why do i dare for her
she's so awesome
passion ignites
why, why, why

dare for her
care for her
should for her
would for her
If i knew, then i could for her
...
dare for her
flair for her
why, why, why

Greener
(happiness where you are)
-inspired by Grant Campbell

i thought it was greener here
i thought it was better there
i traveled a thousand years
to protect myself from lack

i found all that life could be
i forgot my complacency
i traveled a thousand seas
to indulge myself in all

i knew there was more to life
i figured i would find it soon
i traveled a thousand thoughts
to find the ultimate place of rest

but now there is no one left
and now all my friends are gone
i'd travel a thousand deaths
to be back where i began

Aaron

Let the wash come over me
Cover me river of strength
I am weary, let me drink
I am dying, let me be

Everyone I know hates me
Get this shit off of my back

Let this noose give up some slack
These damn tears won't let me see

There is nothing I can't do
There is no one who can say
You can't help me anyway
You can't play me for the fool

Fools and demons all the same
Each one spitting in my face
All that shit goes to the grave
Even assholes know my name

I'll run away ~~~ And die
I'll run away ~~~ I'll fly
I'll run away ~~~ Won't cry
I'll run away ~~~ Don't try

And stop me

My Captain

You are Jehovah the almighty Rock of Ages.
Fortress of faith. Towering wonder.

Your castle is high and Impregnable, Impenetrable, Immovable.
Your warehouses are full and overflowing.

Your streams are uncrossable.
The Leviathan hides your treasures.

A safe refuge in time of trouble.
You are my rampart, my battlement, my cairn, my fort.

Your archers can split a hair in two.
Your fiery chariots are no match for anyone.

You assemble your army from among the stones,
So that no one may march against you.

You establish your castle forever on your isle of glass.

Camelot, no... Heaven is your dwelling place.

And to you do I run.

You are the General and the Captain of the Faith.

One Christ

Fifty stout warriors clad in mail.
all wielding spears, waiting to prevail.
One hundred horsemen riding
their awesome beasts of war.
Lances shields and armor
shinning they adorn.
One thousand archers set
in an impregnable fort.
piercing careless soldiers
finding game to sport.
Ten thousand chariots gleaming,
ten thousand riders strong.
An army in an army,
so great alone the throng.
One million footmen ready,
with sword and shield and mail.
All ready for their death that day
or waiting to prevail.

One newborn babe, a precious boy
    not a mighty man at all.
One God, One man, one Christ the lamb

stands more powerful than all.

<pre>
a poem to hold next to your heart,
     so it may rest upon your soul
</pre>

a smile here
a note there
a little love
for to share

your deep brown eyes
cannot disguise
your heart within
my spirit swims

the sounding laugh
your golden hair
no lonely path
for me to fare

a gentle touch
a deep warm hug
honey so true
may I come to you?

NQA

I didn't know of anyone else
To hide my pain... my ruin so great
Plunge it deep within the earth
If I must then I will, NQA
So heavy a weight. Pain. Shoulders.
I'm getting that sinking... again...

Shadows play off of her imagination
I am dancing as by firelight
A tickle, fickle trickle of hope
A respite from the world, NQA
Will I go down to the sea I wonder
Will she ever go down with me

Mighty crashing these forests tell of
But who will be there to listen
Who is there to hear my faith fall
She is to me the ear of reason: NQA
But if I am tied to her so well
Why the kite? Why so long a string

Will she love me
Will I love back
NQA
No Questions Asked
Will she like me
Another Matter Entirely
AME

Spontaneous Psalm #6

Take away all my sadness
Till the skys fall from heaven
Till the stars fall on my head
Take it away

I think that's till the end
I don't know
I don't care
It's so sublime

God: maker of all the earth
And my heart

Well I just want to be yours
I just want to be yours

Till the skys fall out of heaven
I want to be yours

Jehovah Tsidkenu
Take me away with you

Jehovah Rapha
I want to love ya

Jehovah Jirah
Jehovah Nissi

Jehovah Shalom
Jehovah Shalom

Adam and Jesus called you Daddy
And here I come too
I run into you daddy
Lord I come to you

Come to you

I tend to think in strange terms... but at what point CAN you actually cut off humankind from their humanness? Or I could ask this: When does a sentient being become a sentient being? At what point is a person actually defined as a person? Is it when the sperm is captured by the egg? Is it when they develop into a fetus? Is it at birth? Or is it perhaps at christening or baptism? Or how about at the age of reasoning when they can differentiate between right and wrong?

I believe that you don't know do you? I think that you are sitting there reading these very words and still do not have any idea your own VIEWS on the subject on Creation, Life, and Abortion. Well, here: let me tell you what others think: In the 1100's, Provision 53 of the Assyrian code declared that any woman who was caught having done an abortion on herself or any woman who had received an abortion, must be impaled on spikes in public view without the dignity of burial. Even later Greeks, Romans, Catholics and Muslims alike agreed separately, that abortion was wrong. In historic Judaism, we find abortion of a child a sin that cannot be tolerated, except that when the mothers life is endangered.

Every doctor that graduated from any major medical school in the United States takes the Hippocratic Oath. Hippocrates stated that Abortion under no circumstances was a just, fair or "right" thing to do... and Every Doctor swears that they will never perform this travesty upon another human. But, they still do it don't they?

Well, the first written law prohibiting abortion anywhere was the Miscarriage of Women act in 1803 published in England. A later act was written in 1828, and again in 1961 and remained in effect until 1968. Even then, it was only in the case where it is a necessary thing if it threatens the mental and physical health of a mother; or if it seems that the child will be born with handicaps. This law applies to everybody except Northern Ireland, where it is still illegal.

Even in 1871 the New York Times called abortion the "Evil of the Age"... The American Medical Association waged war against it via literature and soliciting. They were quoted saying that "She (women) yields to the pleasures - but shrinks from the pains and responsibilities of maternity... She sinks into old age like a withered tree, stripped of its foliage, with the stain of blood upon her soul, she dies without the hand of affection to smooth her pillow."

So tell me... What are your views? I would like to know...
And for Gods sake... what exactly happened in the 60's? And don't give me this bullshit story about free love and all that. I'll tell you what happened. We rejected the teachings of our Lord Christ and Savior by allowing this injustice to flush through our souls like fouled sewage. We have seen the pustulating corpse of Abortion in its true form of pre-meditated slaughter and did naught but winked... We have drank the urine of society and pretended not to notice.

I notice. And I tend to think that God does too.

The Berean Thing

Paul Bradley Hart, Comedian to Ethiopia.

At least that's what I told Tracy, Eldon, Luke, and Chris one day in Bible class. After the laughter subsided, I told them: "Or something to bring laughter to the hurting world." And, to that degree, I am not far off. Now, with the big 5-0 in the near future, I look back and wonder: "Was I that far off?"

So, quick thirty year recap - College was seminary, then two pastoral jobs, then wound up owning a Christian Coffee Shop and a Magazine. Divorce... Ugh... Then... Divorce... Ugh... Then became an artist. Worked in Dance, Theater, Live Music, Fine Arts, Fine Art Teaching, Music again, and finally landed on writing. Here I am, thirty years later, a writer. Imagine Ms. Wright's surprise.

Now, if I would have stuck to something maybe I would be a "success" or maybe I would be "rich" - but snorkeling in the Caribbean, I asked myself the same question and it was always: "NAH." I'm glad to have wasted years on following the "Next Big Thing" and not anchoring myself to a moor.

Until I met Jennifer, Wife #Forever (read: #3) and things are just dandy thank you very much. We flip houses and have some degree of wealth. But, mind you, it took me a long time to understand what all the fuss was about. Not worrying about a "cuddle-buddy" is among the first. A good wife... Who can find one? I did... Praise Jesus.

And were all those weird years wasted? Did I throw it all away managing coffee shops and convenience stores and making donuts and running janitorial businesses and cleaning windows and paving driveways and running a mall kiosk? Nope. I look at all those experiences and chock it up to: "Growth." See, growing up with Prune Belly Syndrome was a horrible curse, and, though you people were nice to me, I was always called "Pregnant" and "Fatty" by all the other kids in Wichita. It was a challenge understanding who I was.

I was and will always be an artist. Being weird was supposed to be normal. I just didn't know that at the time. It wasn't until I was 21 that I could look myself in the mirror and say: "I love you." And that's the Jesus part. When I was fresh out of seminary, I waited for Mrs. Hart to come along, and I saved my body for her. 25 LONG years I waited. Hey, I ain't no Wesley or Quincey with dashing good looks, but there were some intriguing offers that I had to say no to. It was easy because I knew "SHE" was in the future and I would wait.

And when Mrs. Hart broke my life in two (abuse, cheating, betrayal, lying) I began to drink and smoke and do drugs and carouse. That crap ain't worth it. Ten years later, at 35, I said: "Enough is enough" and got back in touch with the Lord. It's a much happier life. Then Jennifer entered and things have been peachy keen ever since. Well... You know, the tales of woe from everyday adventures on earth aside, peachy keen, nonetheless. A threefold cord cannot easily be broken.

So... If I were to look back at little old Paul telling Tracy, Eldon, Luke, and Chris about his aspirations... I wouldn't change a thing. The heart was true and I meant it. I really do still desire to bring hope to the hopeless and peace to the distraught. As I am fond of saying: "I'm just a nobody, trying to tell anybody, about a somebody, who loves everybody."

And I do. Whether it's through song or the written word, I tell people that Jesus loves them and has a wonderful plan for their life... I also tell them that

Satan hates them and has a horrible plan for their life... And it's up for them to choose one or the other.

Choose life. Choose Jesus.

High School Outcast

Going to a public school changed me however. Two of the science teachers were also sponsors of our Bible Club as well as the Bible Study. Each Tuesday morning, my dad would drive me to school early so we could have our Bible study. One of the teachers also taught geology. My father was a geologist so I did just fine in that class, and one morning in Bible Study we asked her to share about her views on the world. Now, this was in 1989 and there was a huge legal battle about See You At The Pole as well as Bibles in the public school setting, so she could only answer questions and not give prepared lessons. Tricky stuff, but she did end up sharing that she had a "Young Earth" view on creation and that the deluge and that there was the possibility of an earth before Genesis 1:1.

I was a little taken aback at this new teaching and dug into it really hard. Eventually I came to understand that the beginning was actually the beginning, but I did subscribe to her reasoning that the earth was young. Only 6,700 years or so. It stood to reason because of verses about Peleg and Noah and reforming of the earth in and around the Deluge. She believed in a planet however so I didn't want to ask her questions about the four corners of the wind or about the foundations of the earth. She did mention the "heavens" and subscribed to a pre-flood canopy theory, which I found pretty really interesting.

As my studies led me deeper and deeper into biblical parts unknown I would continually wrestle with certain concepts that C.S. Lewis taught me. And I'm not talking about Eustace Clarence Scrubb and his love of dragon treasure. Unknown to many a reader, Lewis wrote a science fiction trilogy in where the earth is described as "The Silent Planet" and how most of our bodies in the Solar System were inhabited with various creatures and beings but only one was silent and the Son of God only died for the one fallen race, and that was the Terrans on earth. This teaching messed me up for decades.

So the more I read the bible the more I would find other texts to read. Jasher and Enoch were at the forefront. Between skateboarding with Wesley or Erin or watching Fletch and Alex work on their vintage Chevys there wasn't a lot of time to read… But when I did read it was usually the Bible. That is, until I started reading science fiction again. I don't know how it happened but it crept up on me. Suddenly I had copies of H.G. Wells, Heinlein, Bova, and Asimov on the shelf. "Oh it's ok. They're not comics." I would tell myself. Soon I was back at it again… "Ok so what if there are other planets and maybe only 1% of them are inhabited?" and questions like that. The book of Genesis was retreating farther and farther into the recesses of my mind and the teachings of ancient galactic civilizations were growing fruit.

"A long time ago in a galaxy far, far away…" was the boldest lie to ever hit the silver screen. I bought into it and millions of others did as well. The love affair that men have with going "outside of upper earth orbit" and colonizing the L5 position of the moon or even having a base on the moon, or getting over to mars and terraforming that ball of red dirt… Ugh. It all came to me that the dogged insistent lies of the ones who create and distribute motion pictures are indeed of Satan. The more and more I read Genesis chapters 1-11, the more and more I recognized something was not right. And by the time I got to seminary, I had a handle on the basics of what I thought the main problem was. For I had at least made the separation when I came back from Harvest Christian. I had burned the "dross" and kept the "gold" - I had allowed myself to see both aspects with perspective. It was this one thing that saved my mind going forward.

www.ingramcontent.com/pod-product-compliance
Lightning Source LLC
Chambersburg PA
CBHW030153200626
46812CB00016B/1831